ROTHERHAM LIBRARIES AND NEIGHBOURHOOD HUBS

This book is worth 2 stars.

Special thanks to Rachel Elliot and Hayley Goleniowska

ORCHARD BOOKS

First published in Great Britain in 2022 by Hodder & Stoughton Limited.

1 3 5 7 9 10 8 6 4 2

© 2022 Rainbow Magic Limited.
© 2022 HIT Entertainment Limited.
Illustrations © 2022 by Hodder & Stoughton Limited.

The moral rights of the author and illustrator have been asserted.
All characters and events in this publication, other than those clearly in the public domain,
are fictitious and any resemblance to real persons, living or dead, is purely coincidental.

A CIP catalogue record for this book is available from the British Library.

ISBN 978 1 40836 709 4

Printed and bound in Great Britain by Clays Ltd, Elcograf S.p.A

The paper and board used in this book are made from wood from responsible sources.

Orchard Books
An imprint of Hachette Children's Group
Part of Hodder & Stoughton Limited
Carmelite House, 50 Victoria Embankment, London EC4Y 0DZ

An Hachette UK Company
www.hachette.co.uk
www.hachettechildrens.co.uk

Harper
the Confidence
Fairy

By Daisy Meadows

ORCHARD

www.orchardseriesbooks.co.uk

Contents

Story One:
The Belief Badge

Story Two:
The Cool Coronet

Story Three:
The Poise Purse

Jack Frost's Spell

The Confidence Fairy is stylish and cool,
But soon she is going to feel like a fool.
Her garland, her poise purse, her cool coronet,
I'll steal them all swiftly and make her upset.

When I have her magic, the humans will kneel.
I'll crush all their confidence under my heel.
Without self-belief they will cower and flee,
And beg for a king who will rule them – that's me!

Story One
The Belief Badge

Chapter One
A Splinter in the Spinney

"I love climbing," said Kirsty Tate, swinging her legs.

She peered down through the leafy branches of the biggest oak tree in the park.

"This is the best thing about the summer holidays," said her best friend,

Rachel Walker. "Climbing trees, having fun, no homework . . ."

"And keeping an eye out for magic," Kirsty added, smiling.

Ever since they had met on Rainspell Island, fairy magic had followed them wherever they went. They had shared all sorts of exciting adventures, and they were always on the lookout for the next one.

"It's lovely to have you staying for a whole week," said Rachel. "I've been looking forward to showing you the Spinney."

The Spinney was the nature park behind Rachel's house. They had leaned their bikes against a tree and climbed to the top so that they could see the little stream that ran through the park.

"How about a paddle in the stream?"

Kirsty suggested. "Then we could unpack our picnic. I'm starving already, and it's only eleven o'clock."

"Good idea," said Rachel, turning to make her way down. "Ouch! Splinter."

She dropped down from the tree and heard a shout of surprise. She had almost landed on a group of children. There was a girl with long dark-brown plaits, a tall boy with glasses and a black-haired boy in an orange wheelchair.

"Sorry," said Rachel, noticing that they all looked rather miserable. "I didn't mean to scare you. I've got a splinter."

She stuck out her thumb, and the boy in the wheelchair winced.

"I can help," he said.

He reached under his chair and took out a first-aid kit. From inside, he pulled tweezers and a plaster. Gratefully, Rachel took them and sat down. Kirsty jumped out of the tree.

"Hi, I'm Kirsty and this is Rachel," said Kirsty.

"I'm Sully," said the boy. "These are my friends Luca and Flora."

"Nice to meet you," said Flora, with a faint smile.

Rachel took a deep breath and pulled out the splinter.

"Got it," she said. "Thanks, Sully."

She put a plaster on her thumb and returned the tweezers. Luca looked at his watch.

"We have to get back to the club," he said to his friends with a sigh.

Rachel and Kirsty exchanged a glance. Why did they seem down in the dumps?

"What's your club?" asked Kirsty.

"It's the Confidence Club," Sully explained. "We were being bullied at our schools, and one day we met here and made friends. And soon lots of other children joined."

"When the weather got colder, we needed somewhere to play," said Flora. "There's an old clubhouse in the middle of the Spinney and the owner let us use it for free."

"Till now," said Luca. "He's selling it, so we have to pack up our things and leave."

The three friends exchanged sad glances. Rachel and Kirsty felt sorry for them.

"We'd love to see it," said Kirsty.

"Of course – come with us," said Flora.

Rachel and Kirsty wheeled their bikes along the path, following Sully towards the centre of the Spinney.

"We teach each other our hobbies and have a go at learning new skills," Flora explained. "And this is where it all happens."

She waved proudly towards a weather-worn wooden cabin. One of the windows was boarded up, and the door had been mended with rough planks of wood.

"It doesn't look like much on the

outside," said Sully. "But come and see
what we've done inside."

When the door opened, Rachel and
Kirsty gasped. The walls had been
painted in bright colours and decorated
with pictures, drawings and quotations.

"We got chairs and tables that people
were throwing away," said Luca. "Flora's
good at woodwork so she mended them."

The floor was covered in colourful rugs, and there was a bookcase filled with old books. Fairy lights were strung around the room and a few chipped cups and plates were stacked neatly on a side table. Flora took a blanket from a pile of fleecy throws and wrapped herself in it.

"This place is fabulous," said Rachel. "I love it."

"So do we," said Sully. "That's why

we're so sad to leave it."

"Could you buy the clubhouse?" asked Kirsty.

Sully, Flora and Luca looked startled.

"We're just kids," said Luca. "We don't have any money."

"And today is when the owner has to make his choice," said Sully. "Whoever offers the most money will get the clubhouse."

"Maybe he'll give you a bit more time," said Kirsty. "You could throw a fundraising party."

"Maybe we could," said Sully with a flicker of hope in his eyes.

"Of course you could," said Rachel. "You just have to believe in yourselves!"

"We can help," said Kirsty. "While you organise the party, we can visit the owner. We'll ask him for extra time so you can try to raise the money."

"Would you really?" asked Flora. "That's so kind."

"Well, you were kind to us," said Rachel with a smile. "We're just returning the favour."

Sully told them the owner's address, and they turned to go. As they passed a tray of broken knick-knacks waiting to

be mended, a little trinket box caught
Kirsty's eye. It was decorated with tiny
jewels that glimmered and glowed . . .
really glowed.

"Rachel," Kirsty whispered in a thrilled
voice. "I think there's magic in the air."

Tingling with excitement, Rachel
picked up the box and they hurried
outside. As soon as they were hidden
behind a large bush, she opened the lid. A
glittering fairy with brown hair smiled up
at them.

"Hi," she said. "I'm Harper the
Confidence Fairy."

Chapter Two
The Confidence Club

"It's lovely to meet you," said Rachel.

Harper was wearing a floaty, pink dress and turquoise glasses that matched her gauzy wings. Her hazel eyes sparkled with fun.

"What do you do?" Kirsty asked.

She knew that every fairy was

responsible for something special.

"I help humans grow their confidence," said Harper. "But today I need help."

"We're always ready to help our fairy friends," said Kirsty.

"What's happened?" asked Rachel.

"I made the mistake of trusting Jack Frost," said Harper miserably. "You see, I have Down's syndrome. It's given me the gift of trusting everyone. That's always been a really good thing – till today."

"What is Down's syndrome?" asked Kirsty.

"We all have tiny instructions called chromosomes inside us," Harper explained. "They control things like the colour of your hair and eyes, or the length of your fingers. Down's syndrome gave me an extra chromosome. It makes me look and learn differently from some other fairies."

"Well, every fairy is different anyway," said Rachel. "Just like every human. It would be awful if everyone were the same!"

Kirsty nodded.

"What has Jack Frost done?" she asked gently.

Harper sighed.

"I was working in my Confidence Lab," she said. "That's where we come up with new ways to help humans, like belief badges that give the wearer a boost of confidence. Anyway, that's when Jack Frost turned up and asked me to tell him about my work."

"What did he want to know?" asked Rachel, with a curious expression.

"He wanted to see my magical objects," said Harper. "So, I showed them to him. I have a heart-shaped belief badge covered in sequins that helps people to love and trust who they are on the inside. Then there's my cool coronet."

"I like the sound of that," said Kirsty.

"It's so pretty," said Harper, smiling. "It's a garland of flowers that encourages people to have faith in sharing their own ideas. My favourite of all is the sparkly poise purse. It helps people to find their own special style that shows their personality."

"Your things sound lovely," said Rachel.

"Thanks," said Harper. "That's what Jack Frost said too . . . just before he grabbed my magical objects and disappeared in a flash of blue lightning."

"What a mean thing to do," said Kirsty, feeling very sorry for the little fairy.

"I came here because I've been watching over Luca, Sully and Flora ever since they started the Confidence Club," Harper went on. "I'm worried about them now that Jack Frost has my magical objects. Confidence all over the human world will start to crumble. Then I saw you two. Queen Titania always says that you're Fairyland's best friends, and I thought you might help me."

"Of course we will," said Rachel.

Chapter Three
The Way to Fairyland

"We have a promise to keep to the Confidence Club," said Kirsty. "But I don't feel very confident about talking to the clubhouse owner."

"Me neither," said Rachel, "I'm not clever enough to say the right thing. We're bound to fail."

"You've stopped trusting yourselves because my belief badge is missing," Harper said. "You won't succeed if you try now. We have to get the belief badge back first. Then you'll be able to keep your promise."

The girls let out long sighs of relief.

"Let's start by looking for Jack Frost," said Rachel, and then she paused and looked at Kirsty. "Does that seem like the right thing to do?"

"Maybe we should go to Queen Titania and ask her," Kirsty suggested. "Or maybe she wouldn't like that. Oh dear, I usually feel a lot more certain than this."

"I find it helps to follow a pattern," said Harper. "What would you usually do to find Jack Frost?"

"We'd start at his home," said Kirsty.

"Then that's where we'll go," said Harper.

She waved her wand around her head, and a flurry of multicoloured sparkles washed over them. The girls shrank to fairy size as their gossamer wings unfurled. Rachel looked at her painful thumb and saw a tiny, fairy-sized plaster  where the splinter had been.

They fluttered upwards with Harper, and the wooden cabin glowed in the light of her fairy dust. She tapped the wall with

the tip of her wand, and it slid sideways.
Instead of seeing the Confidence Club
on the other side, a bright, magical glow
beamed from the gap.

The fairies flew into the light, and for
a moment the magical glow was all they
could see. Then, seconds later, they were
hovering above the Ice Castle. It looked
as grim and forbidding as ever, even
though it was blanketed in thick snow.
Icicles hung from every windowsill and
frost made the bare trees glitter.

"Oh my goodness, there he is!" Kirsty
exclaimed.

She pointed to the main castle entrance,
where Jack Frost was talking to three
goblins. The fairies flew as close as they
dared and ducked behind a frosted shrub.

"The trouble with humans and fairies

is that they don't know what's good for them," Jack Frost was ranting as he paced up and down. "Me! I'm better than all of them."

"But how are you going to teach them that?" asked the first goblin, who was wearing a mustard-yellow bandana around his neck.

"We've met these goblins before," Rachel whispered. "They're dreadfully mischievous. They caused a lot of trouble when we were with Maryam the Nurse Fairy."

"Easy peasy fairy squeezy," snarled Jack Frost. "I'm going to crush their self-confidence. Then they'll admire me because I can tell them all what to do."

"You're a genius, my lord," said the goblin with the lime-green bandana.

"Yes, you're a wonder," added the third goblin, whose bandana was rust-orange.

"Stop flattering me and start being useful," Jack Frost yelled. "Now I've got these, I can destroy confidence in everyone except ME."

He held out three items in his hands, and Harper gave a little yelp.

"Those are mine," she whispered. "They're my magical objects!"

Chapter Four
Jack Frost's Worst Goblins

Jack Frost tossed one magical object to each goblin.

"Hide them in the human world," he ordered. "I'm giving you just enough magic to get to your hiding places. Then you're on your own. Don't fail!"

He turned and stalked back into the

castle, while the goblins sniggered and rubbed their hands together.

"No feeble fairy is a match for us," said the goblin with the rust-orange bandana. "We're going to make these things impossible to find."

They shared a high five and the goblin with the lime-green bandana yelped.

"Ouch, that stung," he complained.

"Baby," snapped the goblin wearing the mustard-yellow bandana. "You wouldn't last five minutes in the forest."

"Is that where you're hiding your coronet?" asked the rust-orange goblin.

"There's a forest faun that owes me a favour," the mustard-yellow goblin replied. "What about you?"

"I'm going to sneak the purse into a dragon's nest in the Fire Mountains," said

the rust-orange goblin. "It'll be epic."

"I'll take this badge to the last living sphinx," said the lime-green goblin. "He loves tricks and riddles."

"Jack Frost will reward us well for this," said the rust-orange goblin.

There were three flashes of blue lightning, and the goblins disappeared. Rachel, Kirsty and Harper exchanged awed looks.

"A dragon, a faun and a sphinx," said Rachel. "This is a real-life quest!"

"Where do we start?" said Kirsty, feeling overwhelmed.

"We can do it," said Harper with certainty in her voice. "I trust you two completely. You've always succeeded before. I know you'll succeed this time."

Her belief in them was so strong that it

made them feel stronger too. They smiled and squeezed each other's hand.

"Luckily, I also know where the sphinx lives," Harper went on.

Grinning, she whooshed her wand. Instantly, the snow and ice were replaced by sand and the heat of the midday sun. They were standing on the edge of a vast desert, overlooking a broad river.

"We're human again," said Kirsty, missing her wings.

"And warm, thank goodness," said Rachel, wincing as her thumb tingled.

The winding river was thronging with vessels of all shapes and sizes. Little boats with curving white sails darted between large, luxurious cruise ships, motorboats and rowing boats.

"Those little ones are called feluccas," said Rachel. "We learned about them in school."

As she stared, she saw a familiar figure wobbling around at one end of a felucca. He had put on a large hat and a cream tunic, but he was still wearing his lime-green bandana.

"Goblin!" Rachel cried. "Come on!"

"Wait," said Harper, who was fluttering between them. "Turn around."

The girls turned and gasped. They were standing in front of a cave, and in the mouth of the cave was the strangest creature they had ever seen. It was the colour of sand, with the head of a pharoah and the body of a lion. Its front paws were crossed, and it was watching them unblinkingly.

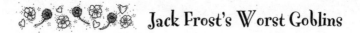
"Rachel, Kirsty," said Harper. "Let me introduce you to the last living sphinx."

Chapter Five
The Last Sphinx

Rachel and Kirsty curtseyed politely.
They weren't sure if this was the right
way to greet a sphinx, but it bowed its
head in return and seemed pleased.

"We are looking for Harper's belief
badge," said Rachel. "It's one of her
magical objects. Have you seen it?"

The sphinx nodded but said nothing.
Rachel and Kirsty exchanged a confused
glance.

"It only answers exact questions," said
Harper, fluttering forwards. "Please, will
you tell me where I can find my badge?"

The sphinx spoke in a deep, rich voice.
"It is in my safekeeping."

"Will you give it to me, please?"

"No."

"Who will you give it to?"

"The first to answer my riddle," said the
sphinx.

There was a loud, squawking yell
behind them, and the goblin came
scrambling up the sand bank.

"How did you find me?" he screeched
at the girls. "It's not fair!"

"We found you fair and square," said

Kirsty. "We have come to get Harper's badge back."

"You shan't have it," the goblin snarled, turning to the sphinx. "You, pharoah face, give me back my badge. I need a better hiding place than you."

The sphinx didn't seem to notice that the goblin was being rude. It shook its noble head.

"Now that you have placed a treasure

in my keeping, you too must answer a riddle to release it."

The goblin yelled and stamped his enormous feet. He yanked on his own ears in fury. He called the sphinx rude names and he threatened that Jack Frost would tell it off. The sphinx closed its eyes and waited. Finally, the goblin stopped squawking.

"Fine, I'll answer your stupid riddle," he muttered. "As long as I can go first."

The sphinx opened its eyes and looked at Harper, Rachel and Kirsty.

"Which one of you will answer my riddle?" he asked.

"We can't," said Kirsty, turning to Rachel in alarm. "How can we answer a riddle set by such a wise, old creature?"

Rachel gazed into her best friend's eyes.

Like Kirsty, she felt fearful. But there was another feeling inside her too, and it was stronger than her fears.

"I don't believe I can do it," she said. "But I do believe in you, Kirsty. As long as we are together, we can do anything."

"You're right," said Harper, hugging Rachel. "That's true friendship."

"I'll answer the riddle," Rachel told the sphinx.

The sphinx looked at the goblin first.

> "I went to the forest and got it.
> I could feel it, but I couldn't find it,
> So I carried it home with me.
> What was it?"

The goblin frowned. "That's impossible," he complained. "It doesn't make sense."

The sphinx was silent.

"Ask me another," the goblin wailed. "That one's not fair. I wasn't ready."

Slowly, the sphinx closed its eyes.

"Fine," said the goblin. "Something I might carry home from the forest. A picnic basket?"

The sphinx shook its head and turned to Rachel. She stared at Kirsty and Harper in dismay. Overhead, a vulture cawed in the silence. Rachel closed her eyes, racking her brains, trying her best. But all she could think about was her throbbing thumb. Why did she have to get that annoying splinter?

The answer hit her like a bolt of Jack Frost's lightning.

"A splinter," she cried triumphantly. "The answer is a splinter!"

Slowly, the sphinx uncrossed its velvety paws and showed them the shining belief badge.

"Yes!" exclaimed Harper, zooming towards the badge.

It shrank to fairy size as soon as she touched it, and she twirled around in pure joy. Rachel and Kirsty wrapped their arms around each other and jumped around in delight. When they looked again, the sphinx and its cave had vanished. Only the goblin remained, glaring at them.

"You've spoiled everything!" he yelled.

Furiously, he turned and stomped back towards the boats. Harper hardly noticed him go. She was beaming with happiness.

"I'll send you back to Tippington," she told the girls. "Then I'll head to Fairyland for some quiet time out before the next part of our quest."

As Harper raised her wand, Rachel and Kirsty squeezed each other's hand.

"I can't believe we met a sphinx," said Kirsty. "I'm never going to forget this adventure."

"Me neither," said Rachel. "And I'm never going to complain about splinters again!"

Story Two
The Cool Coronet

Chapter Six
Save Our Clubhouse

Kirsty and Rachel went spinning through the air in a sparkling whirl of fairy dust. One moment they were waving to Harper in the desert, and the next they were standing in a narrow, shadowy alleyway. The sparkles faded and the girls looked around.

"We're human again," said Kirsty. "But where are we?"

"I know this place," said Rachel. "We're back in Tippington, next to the office where the clubhouse owner works."

"And look, we've got transport," added Kirsty, spotting their bikes leaning against the wall. "We're exactly where we need to be."

Leaving the bikes in the alleyway, they went into the building. The owner's name was printed on a glass door in bold letters: Ian Elliot. Rachel knocked on the door.

"Come in," said a deep voice.

Inside, a man was sitting at a large, polished wooden desk. He had long, white hair, and a clipped white beard.

"Can I help you?" he asked, looking slightly surprised.

"I'm Kirsty Tate," Kirsty began. "And this is my best friend, Rachel Walker."

"We met the children who use your clubhouse today," Rachel went on.

"Ah yes, the Confidence Club," said Mr Elliot, smiling.

"We feel sorry that they're going to lose the clubhouse," Kirsty added. "They have worked so hard to make it special."

"I'm sorry too," said Mr Elliot. "But I am moving away from Tippington. Whoever offers me the most money by midday will be the new owner."

Rachel took a deep breath and gathered up all her courage.

"We wondered if you could wait a

little longer," she said in a small voice. "Sully, Luca and Flora are trying to raise enough money to buy it."

"Pardon?" asked Mr Elliot in astonishment. "How can children find that sort of money?"

"We know they can do it," said Kirsty enthusiastically. "They just need a bit more time."

"You obviously have great confidence in them," said Mr Elliot, smiling.

He put his fingertips together. The girls waited in silence. They could tell that he was thinking hard.

"All right," said Mr Elliot at last. "I will give them until midnight tonight. If they have the money by the time the clock strikes twelve, they can buy the clubhouse. If not, I will have to sell it to someone else."

The girls exchanged a glance.
Midnight! That didn't give them much
time.

"Thank you, Mr Elliot," said Kirsty.
"Come on, Rachel. We have to tell the
others straight away!"

They collected their bikes from the

alleyway and raced back to the clubhouse in the Spinney. Luca, Sully and Flora were delighted to hear the news.

"You've both been amazing," Sully said, beaming at them. "Thank you so much."

"I've made some posters," said Luca. "Sully delivered them around Tippington."

"My aunt works at Radio Tippington,"

said Flora. "She's asked listeners to donate food and decorations, or to pay for a ticket to the fundraising party."

"And my brother is going to play some

music for us," added Luca. "He's in a band."

"We're going to have the party here at dusk," Sully went on. "Will you help us to get ready, Rachel and Kirsty?"

"Definitely," said Rachel, unwrapping her sandwiches. "Just as soon as we've eaten our sandwiches. I'm starving!"

Chapter Seven
The Confidence Lab

A steady stream of people began to arrive at the clubhouse. First, Luca's brother came with his band and their instruments. Then local people started to bring donations for the party. The tables were soon filling up with bowls of fruit, plates of buns, pies, cakes, flans and sandwiches, and bottles of pop, juice and cordial. Decorations piled up in the corner, and the band practised at the back of the clubhouse.

"People are so kind and generous," said Flora, looking through a box of fairy lights.

"There are paper stars that hang from the ceiling here," said Kirsty, who was examining another box.

"We should probably spread the food out across all the tables," Rachel suggested.

Everyone nodded . . . but no one moved.

"How should we organise the food?" asked Luca.

"What's the best way to set out the tables?" Flora wondered aloud.

"Maybe we should start by hanging up the lights," said Kirsty. "Or should the lights come last?"

"Luca, where do you want the band to play?" his brother called.

"How shall we sell the tickets?" Sully asked.

No one had any answers. The children stared at each other.

"I don't know what's best," said Kirsty.

"I can't make up my mind either," Rachel added.

"How can we set up an amazing party when none of us knows what looks good?" said Kirsty.

"This is happening because Harper's cool coronet is missing," said Rachel in a low voice. "We've all lost faith in our own ideas."

"We have to find that coronet before the party," Kirsty replied. "The goblin with the mustard-yellow bandana said that he was taking it to a forest faun."

"But which forest did he mean?" asked Rachel. "And which faun?"

"We have to find Harper," said Kirsty.

"Perhaps she can help us to find the faun before it's too late."

The girls slipped out of the clubhouse while the others were trying to decide how to build a stage for the band. Inside each of their lockets was just enough fairy dust to carry them to Fairyland. The lockets had been a gift from Queen Titania, and they were Rachel and Kirsty's greatest treasures.

"Quickly," said Rachel, fumbling with the catch. "Hurry before someone sees us."

Eagerly, the girls held hands and sprinkled themselves with the glittering fairy dust.

"Take us to Harper, please," said Kirsty.

With a magical tingle, they transformed into fairies. A flash of light dazzled them,

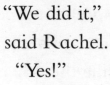

and they blinked.
"We did it,"
said Rachel.
"Yes!"
They were
inside a
vast, open
workshop
with walls
of red, yellow,
blue, green and
orange. Gleaming
white desks were dotted here and there,
among intricate machines with shining
cogs and wheels. Fairies were all around
them, using machines, drawing designs
and testing spells.

There was a squeal, and a dark-haired
fairy threw her arms around them.

"Rachel!" she exclaimed. "Kirsty! Oh my goodness, welcome to the Confidence Lab!"

"Eleanor the Snow White Fairy!" said Kirsty,

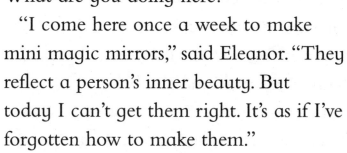

hugging her back. "It's great to see you. What are you doing here?"

"I come here once a week to make mini magic mirrors," said Eleanor. "They reflect a person's inner beauty. But today I can't get them right. It's as if I've forgotten how to make them."

"Do you think it's because two of

Harper's objects are still missing?" asked
Rachel.

"I'm sure it is," said Eleanor.
"Everyone's having problems."

She looked around. Amelia the Singing
Fairy was frowning over a bowl of
sparkling fairy dust. Ivy the Worry Fairy
was pacing up and down, muttering to
herself.

"Amelia's 'finding your voice' spell
keeps going wrong because her hands are
shaking," Eleanor went on. "And poor
Ivy keeps muddling up her magic words.
Thank goodness you're here – I know
things will get better now."

"We hope so," said Rachel.

She felt unsure when she thought about
how much trust the fairies had in them.
What if they failed?

"Follow me," said Eleanor. "I'll take you to Harper."

Chapter Eight
A Magical Map

They saw more fairies they knew as they walked through the lab. No one looked very happy.

"Poor Clare the Caring Fairy," said Eleanor as they passed her. "People aren't sure how to care for others any more."

Phoebe the Fashion Fairy had her head

in her hands.
"There's
Florence," said
Kirsty, waving.
The
Friendship
Fairy didn't see
her. She screwed
up a piece of paper
and threw it into the
recycling bin.

"She's spent
all morning
trying to write
a charm
that makes
friends boost
each other's
confidence," said

Eleanor. "I've never seen her struggle like this."

"There's Harper," said Rachel, darting forwards.

The Confidence Fairy was sitting at a rainbow-coloured desk, in front of rows of colourful, sparkly hairclips. As soon as she saw Rachel and Kirsty, she jumped up and twirled around.

"How lovely of you to come and
see me," she said happily. "I was just
organising my hairclip collection. It
usually calms me down, but not today."

"Why not?" asked Kirsty.

"My favourite clips are missing," said
Harper, her smile fading. "I keep them in
the poise purse, so Jack Frost has them."

"If anyone can help you to get them
back, it's Rachel and Kirsty," said Eleanor,
smiling.

"We came because neither us nor our
Confidence Club friends could decide how
to organise the fundraising party," said
Kirsty.

"We thought it must be because the cool
coronet is missing," Rachel added. "We
have to find the forest faun and see if the
goblin took the coronet to him."

Harper nodded.

"The forest faun?" asked Eleanor. "Snow White knows him. He's lots of fun."

"Could you tell us where he is?" asked Kirsty, holding her breath.

"I can do better than that," said Eleanor.

She waved her wand
and a golden scroll
appeared in Harper's
hand.

"This map will
take you to him,"
Eleanor said. "The
forest is in the human
world, but a few
magical creatures
still live there."

"Thank you," said Harper. "Rachel and
Kirsty, lay your hands on the scroll."

As soon as they did, it glowed brightly
and began to spin. The fairies held on to
it as it turned faster and faster.

The Confidence Lab and Eleanor's
smiling face became a colourful blur.
Then everything went green. They slowed

to a stop and found themselves fluttering among the treetops of a mighty forest.

"Wow," said Harper, grinning. "That was the best fun!"

She fluttered down to the forest floor like a twirling sycamore seed.

"Let's look at the map," said Rachel,

landing lightly beside her.

They opened the scroll, and a golden, dotted line glowed on the map.

"Do you think we have to follow it?" asked Kirsty.

Harper pointed at the scroll with her wand, and it floated in front of them.

"Yes," she said, smiling. "What fun!"

Chapter Nine
A Stripy Friend

The fairies fluttered on, weaving around dapple trees and among tangled vines. The map floated ahead of them, guiding the way.

"The forest is so pretty," said Harper, gazing around in wonder. "I love all the colours of nature."

"How much further?" asked Kirsty, speeding up to see the map more closely. "I feel as if we've been flying for hours."

"It's hard to tell," said Rachel. "Harper, can you – oh! Where is she?" They looked around, their hearts thumping. Where was their friend? Had Jack Frost or one of his goblins grabbed her? A bubbling laugh filled the air, and they heaved sighs of relief. Harper was sitting on the forest floor beside a young badger.

"Come and meet my new friend," she

said. "This is Arnold."

"It's lovely to meet you, Arnold," said Kirsty. "But Harper, we have to find the faun. Every second counts if the fundraising party is going to work."

"I know," said Harper. "But I can't fly for long without getting tired. I had to rest, and then I met Arnold."

She yawned and leaned back against Arnold's stripy, warm body. Suddenly, Rachel had a brainwave.

"Perhaps Arnold could help us," she suggested. "If he would give you a lift, you could carry on making friends as we look for the faun."

Arnold nodded, and Harper lay sleepily on his back.

Now Rachel and Kirsty had to fly close to the ground. For a while, the

only sound was the scuffle and crunch of leaves and pinecones as Arnold shambled onwards.

"Rachel, I'm worried," said Kirsty at

last. "This is taking a long time. Perhaps we shouldn't have come."

"What if this is the wrong forest?" said Rachel.

"Try not to worry," said Harper, who was sitting up on Arnold's back. "We are bound to feel unsure until we find the cool coronet. All we can do is trust each other and keep going."

Arnold let out a loud, snuffly snort and Harper laughed.

"You see, Arnold agrees with me."

Rachel and Kirsty smiled too. Somehow, Harper had a knack for making everyone around her feel better.

A few minutes later, they reached a place where the path split into two.

"Oh dear," said Rachel. "The map doesn't show which way to go."

The golden dots on the map flickered and faded. Then the scroll rolled itself up and melted into thin air. The three fairies exchanged alarmed looks.

"What are we going to do now?" asked Kirsty. "We're completely lost."

Chapter Ten
The Faun's Challenge

Arnold snorted and took the path that led to the right, lumbering over roots and mulch. Rachel and Kirsty followed, and Harper glanced over her shoulder at them.

"Let's trust him," she said. "After all, he knows the forest."

A few minutes later, the trees became
less crowded and they saw a little glade,
carpeted with lush green grass. A faun
was sitting cross-legged in the centre
of the glade, playing a flute. His eyes
were closed. Perhaps he was focusing on
his music. Or perhaps he was trying to
ignore the goblin in front of him, who
was stamping his feet and yelling.

"Give it back!" squawked the goblin, tugging on his mustard-yellow bandana. "It's not fair. I wasn't ready."

As the fairies entered the glade, the faun opened his eyes.

"Hello, Arnold," he said. "What are you doing with all these fairies?"

"We've come to find the cool coronet," said Rachel. "Eleanor the Snow White Fairy told us where to find you."

"What trickery is this?" the goblin screeched, his eyes almost popping out of his head. "Did you tell them where I am? You're on their side!"

"I am not," said the faun, raising one eyebrow. "I have no idea who they are."

"I'm Kirsty," said Kirsty, "and these are my friends Rachel and Harper. We've come because this goblin took Harper's

cool coronet, and we need to get it
back before the whole world runs out of
confidence. Do you have it?"

"I do," said the faun, as the goblin
snarled. "This noisy green person asked
me to protect it with my magic."

"You're a cheat and a liar," the goblin
snapped, sticking out his bottom lip and
folding his arms.

"That is not true," said the faun in a
polite voice. "To get the coronet you only
have to copy my dance exactly. It isn't
my fault if you can't remember it."

"May we see the dance?" asked Rachel.

The faun sprang to his feet in a
twinkling. He twirled, leapt and swayed
all around them, then bowed and smiled.

"That was very complicated," said
Rachel, frowning.

She remembered the first few steps, but then froze, forgetting if the next step went left or right. The faun shook his head.

Next, Kirsty flew forwards. She did a little better than Rachel, but then she lost her balance and fell with a bump.

"See, no one can do it," the goblin grumbled. "He's made it impossible."

"We're not giving up," said Kirsty, brushing herself down.

"Wait," said Harper. "Learning dance

routines is one of my favourite things!"

She sprang down from Arnold's back, curtseyed to the faun, and then began to dance. After the first few steps, the faun gave a little smile and raised his flute. His music echoed around them as Harper danced. Happiness streamed through her, and every twirl and sway overflowed with joy. She was brimming with confidence.

At last the final note rang out, and Harper finished the dance with another curtsey. The faun smiled at her, and played a little flourish of magical notes on his flute. At once, a coronet of flowers appeared on his head. He handed them to Harper with a bow.

"That was beautiful," he said. "I have never seen anyone dance like that."

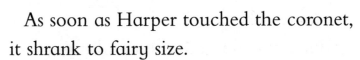

As soon as Harper touched the coronet, it shrank to fairy size.

"Thank you," she whispered.

The goblin let
out a howl of
pure rage
and flung
himself
on to the
ground,
kicking
and
thumping his
arms and legs, and
wailing at the top of his voice.

"We did it!" Harper exclaimed,
throwing her arms around Rachel and
Kirsty.

"You did it," said Kirsty. "Neither of us
can dance like you."

"But I wouldn't have found this place
without you," said Harper, smiling. "We

all have our different strengths."

She waved her wand and the girls'
wings disappeared.
In a dizzying rush,
they returned to
human size.

"I'll send you back
to Tippington now,"
said Harper. "The
fundraising party is
about to begin, and
I must take the cool
coronet home to
Fairyland. But I will see you again
very soon."

Her wand swished once more, and
multicoloured sparkles filled the air.
Through the blur of fairy dust, they
saw the forest faun waving and the

goblin stamping his feet. Then they
were standing behind the clubhouse in
the Spinney. They could hear the band
playing inside, and a hubbub of chatter
and laughter. Rachel and Kirsty shared a
hopeful smile.

"That sounds good," said Kirsty.

They hurried back inside. The tables
had been arranged around the edges of

the room, with a selection of food, drinks and scrumptious cakes and sweets. The band was playing on a makeshift stage, and Luca, Flora and Sully were busily putting up the final decorations.

"How about stringing some fairy lights among the trees outside?" said Rachel.

"Yes, great idea," said Flora. "I'll help."

Suddenly, making decisions felt easy! Kirsty set up a ticket table. Working as a team, they soon finished putting up the decorations.

"Now all we need is visitors," said Flora. "Fingers crossed that lots of people heard about us on the radio."

"Fingers crossed that they want to help us," added Sully.

Kirsty leaned close to her best friend.

"And fingers crossed that we can find the poise purse before midnight," she whispered.

"Have confidence in us," Rachel replied. "After all, we've beaten Jack Frost twice today already. We just have to do it one last time!"

Story Three
The Poise Purse

Chapter Eleven
Nothing to Wear

"Everything looks perfect," said Kirsty happily.

It was a warm summer evening. The scent of flowers floated on the breeze. Rachel, Kirsty and the members of the Confidence Club had worked hard and the party was ready. The trees around the clubhouse glimmered with fairy lights and everything was bathed in the glow of the setting sun.

"Oh look, our first guests," said Flora as a family group walked towards them.

She hurried forwards to greet them. More people appeared and soon Flora, Sully and Luca were busy meeting their visitors and showing them the clubhouse. A teenage girl walked past in a pretty purple dress.

"Everyone looks so smart," said Rachel.

"Yes, not like me," said Kirsty. "I'm covered in sand from the desert and grass stains from the forest."

"Me too," said Rachel with a sigh. "We don't fit in here."

Everywhere they looked, people were wearing their best clothes. The girls shared a miserable glance.

"We don't look as smart as everyone else," said Kirsty. "We're not dressed for a party."

"Let's go back to my house and get changed," said Rachel. "If we go on our bikes we can be there and back in a flash."

The girls sped back to Rachel's house. As soon as they reached Rachel's room,

they flung open her wardrobe doors.

"How about that spotty skirt over my stripy jeans?" asked Rachel.

"I'm not sure," said Kirsty. "There's a nice party dress here. Maybe I could wear it with wellies?"

"Maybe," said Rachel. "Or you could

borrow this unicorn onesie."

The girls looked at each other.

"I have no idea what I want to wear," said Kirsty. "Nothing seems right."

"I can't even think what proper party clothes look like," said Rachel. "My thoughts are all muddled."

"It must be because Harper's poise purse is still missing," Kirsty exclaimed suddenly. "Remember, Rachel? It helps people to find a special style that reflects their personality. We can't choose what to wear because we've lost the confidence to know our own style."

"You're right," said Rachel with a gasp. "But we have to try. We can't miss the party. We're supposed to be running the donations stand, and that's a really important job."

They tried on outfit after outfit. The pile of clothes on the bed grew higher and higher. This one was too babyish. That one was too serious. This one was too purple. This one didn't have enough spots. Everything in Rachel's wardrobe seemed wrong.

"Nothing makes me feel like me," said Kirsty.

At last, the wardrobe was empty and the girls peeped at each other over the pile of clothes on the bed. Feeling miserable, they pulled on the clothes they had been wearing all day. They walked over to the mirror and stood side by side, staring at their reflections.

"How can we make ourselves look better?" Rachel asked.

As Kirsty shrugged her shoulders,

something amazing happened. Glowing letters appeared on the glass.

"They're burning like fire!" Kirsty exclaimed.

You look fabulous
JUST THE WAY
YOU ARE!

The girls were pulled towards the
mirror as if by an invisible rope. The
letters grew big … massive … gigantic …
The girls gasped and covered their eyes …

Chapter Twelve
Mountain Meeting

For a moment, the friends thought they had been magicked into a sauna. The heat was smothering.

"Oh Kirsty, look," Rachel exclaimed as soon as she opened her eyes.

Kirsty gasped. They were standing on a tree-lined mountain path and everything

was bathed in a flaming orange light. Glowing mountains towered around them.

"It's as if they're on fire," said Kirsty.

"Exactly right," said a happy voice behind them.

Rachel and Kirsty whirled around and saw Harper smiling at them.

"Welcome to the Fire Mountains," she said.

"I've never seen anything like it,"

said Kirsty in wonder. "Goodness, I've only just realised: we're fairies again!"

She and Rachel fluttered their shimmering wings and hugged Harper.

"I used all the magic I could find to bring you here," said Harper, who was a little breathless from the effort. "This is where the dragon lives – the one who has my poise purse."

Rachel and Kirsty remembered that the goblin with the rust-orange bandana had talked about sneaking the purse into a dragon's nest.

"Will you help me to try to get it back?" Harper went on.

"We'll be by your side all the way," Rachel promised her, looking up at the colossal mountain they had to climb.

"And it's going to be a long way," Kirsty added.

Holding hands, the three fairies rose into the air and began to fly upwards. It was tiring, even though they were not

on foot. They were so high up that the
air was thin, and they were soon out of
breath.

"Listen," said Rachel a few minutes
later. "Can you hear footsteps?"

They fluttered down to the path.
Someone was rushing down the
mountain path towards them. Their
hearts thumped in excitement as the steps

grew louder. Then
a goblin in a rust-
orange bandana
came skipping
around the bend.
He skidded to a halt
when he saw them.

"Ha ha, too late,"
he gloated. "You
might as well give
up and go home."

"I'll never give up," Harper declared,
lifting up her chin.

"Foolish fairy," said the goblin with a
sneer. "I gave that bad-tempered dragon
the purse, which it loved because all
dragons like glittery things. There's no way
you can get it back now."

He cackled with mean laughter.
Harper looked at Rachel and Kirsty
with a worried expression.

"Don't listen to him," said Kirsty. "He's
just trying to frighten you."

"You might as well fly home and cry to Queen Titania," the goblin went on, mockingly. "I found the worst-tempered dragon in the whole of Fairyland. It's always landing in Goblin Grotto and waving its scaly arms around, trying to grab us. Now that we've given it a present, we won't be in danger any more."

He turned to go, but Rachel blocked his way.

"Please," she said. "You've caused so much trouble. Wouldn't you rather do something kind for once?"

The goblin stared at her and then burst into fresh laughter.

"You feeble fairies don't understand," he retorted. "Mischief is fun!"

Still cackling, he pushed her out of the

way and skipped off down the
mountain path. The fairies
watched him go, and
then looked up at the
glowing mountain.
"It's a long
way to the
top," said
Harper.

Rachel and Kirsty felt doubt clutching at their hearts. The confidence they had felt a moment ago was ebbing away.

"Kirsty, I've got a bad feeling about this," Rachel whispered. "How can we persuade a dragon to give up its treasure?"

"I don't know," said Kirsty, squeezing Rachel's hand comfortingly. "But we have to try!"

Chapter Thirteen
The Dragon's Cave

It seemed even more tiring to fly up the mountain than it had before they met the goblin. With every flutter of their wings, they felt more worried about what they were flying towards. When they were about halfway up, Harper faltered and then floated down to the path.

"It's too far," she said, hanging her head. "Perhaps we should give up. Even if we find it, how can we change the dragon's mind?"

Rachel and Kirsty landed beside her.

"We mustn't lose confidence," said Rachel. "That's what Jack Frost wants."

"Let's walk for a bit," said Kirsty. "You know, soldiers sometimes sing marching songs to help keep them going when they're on a mission. Maybe it would work for us."

The three fairies linked arms, with Harper in the middle. The Confidence Fairy's head drooped, and Rachel and Kirsty shared a determined glance. They had to keep her spirits up.

"Ready?" said Kirsty. "Right foot forward, and ..."

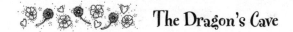

They started to march and sing:

"Oh, the grand old Duke of York,
He had ten thousand men.
He marched them up to the top
of the hill
And he marched them down again."

Harper's head lifted a little, and she started to join in.

"And when they were up they were up,
And when they were down they
were down,
And when they were only halfway up
They were neither up nor down!"

By the end of the
song, Harper
was singing
just as loudly
as Rachel
and Kirsty.
Laughing, she
tossed back her
silky brown hair.
"I needed that,"

she said. "Come on, what other songs shall we sing?"

They were halfway through "The Ants Go Marching", when the mountain path opened up into a wide area where they could rest. Gratefully, they sat down and rubbed their feet.

"I'm glad I'm a fairy and not a soldier," said Harper, smiling. "Marching is much more tiring than flying."

I think it's getting even hotter," said Kirsty, mopping her forehead with her handkerchief. My back feels as if it's on fire."

"Mine too," said Rachel.

"Mine three," said Harper.

They looked at each other, and then slowly turned around. The opening of a dark cave yawned behind them.

"The heat's coming from inside the cave," said Kirsty, not quite sure why she was whispering.

Something was glittering in the entrance. Harper darted forwards and

picked up
handfuls of gold,
silver and jewels.
Necklaces,
bracelets, rings
and tiaras
poured through
her fingers.

"Pretty, shiny
treasures," she
said. "These are
just the sort of
things I like to
keep in my poise
purse."

The three fairies knelt on the treasure,
gasping as emeralds, rubies and diamonds
twinkled at them. They didn't notice
the faint scrape of claws on stone. They

didn't notice the slither of a heavy tail.

"*ROAAARRR!*"

A jet of orange flame shot between them, and they all tumbled backwards. Their hearts pounded with fear and

shock as they scrambled to their feet. From within the depths of the cave, two angry yellow eyes were glaring at them.

"We're v-very sorry," said Rachel at once. "We were only l-looking at your lovely treasures."

There was a louder scrape of claws and an enormous, scaly dragon appeared out of the darkness. Spikes lined its spine, and its lashing tail ended in an arrow-shaped point.

"H-hello," said Kirsty. "We are here to ask—"

"P-please," Rachel tried. "We only want to—"

The next jet of fire ignited a small bush outside the cave.

"No wonder these mountains glow if they're full of dragons setting fire to things," Rachel whispered.

Smoke curled from the dragon's nostrils.

"Oh my goodness, what are we going to do?" asked Kirsty.

"It's so beautiful," said Harper, who didn't seem at all scared. "Look at how its scales shimmer and change colour in the light, from green to blue."

The dragon shook its head again and fire licked the ground. The fairies stumbled backwards.

"We didn't mean to upset you," Rachel called out. "Could we just explain—"

The dragon bared its gleaming white teeth and roared.

"It's almost as if it can't understand us," said Kirsty.

"Or," said Harper suddenly, "as if it can't hear us."

Before Rachel or Kirsty could stop her,
Harper zoomed forwards and landed

inches away from the dragon.

"Harper, come back!" Rachel cried. "You're in danger!"

Chapter Fourteen
A Sign for Help

Harper took no notice. Instead, she locked eyes with the dragon and started to make unusual movements with her hands.

"What are you doing?" called Rachel. "Are you OK?"

"I'm fine," said Harper, not taking her

eyes off the dragon. "I'm using a special kind of sign language called Makaton. It's a way to communicate with someone whose brain understands things in a different way from yours."

The dragon had sat up straight as soon as Harper started to sign. It put its head on one side.

"It looks just like Buttons when he's trying to understand something," said Rachel, thinking of her beloved dog.

"At least its not setting fire to things any more," said Kirsty with relief.

Now it was nodding and making movements with its scaly front feet. Smoke was no longer swirling from its nostrils, and its eyes didn't look so angry.

"I think it's working," said Rachel, clapping her hands.

Harper turned and gave them a smile that lit up her face.

"The dragon knows Makaton too! She's just told me that she is only bad-tempered because she's lonely," Harper explained. "She has been trying to make friends with the

137

goblins, but they didn't understand her signs and she didn't understand that they were scared of her."

"Oh, the poor thing," said Rachel, all her fear melting away. "Maybe you could teach the goblins Makaton."

Harper's smile grew even wider. She signed the idea to the dragon, who nodded eagerly.

"I've promised to explain everything to the goblins and give them Makaton lessons," said Harper. "She is terribly grateful."

The dragon scraped at her treasure. Then she lifted one scaly claw, and the fairies saw a sparkling purse dangling from it.

"My poise purse!" Harper shouted happily. "Oh thank you!"

But as she reached out to take it, there was a blinding flash of blue lightning. Jack Frost appeared and snatched the purse from the dragon.

"You shan't have it!" he snarled at Harper. "I can use this to steal the confidence of every human and fairy. Finally, everyone will agree that I am the best!"

"That's not going to happen," said Rachel, folding her arms.

"Why are you always so mean?" Kirsty added.

But Harper held up her hand and gently shook her head at them.

"Don't be too hard on him," she said. "I understand how you feel, Jack Frost. I am the Confidence Fairy after all, and I know that you only took my things because you lack confidence. Underneath, you don't want to be mean."

"That's not true," Jack Frost blustered. "And I'm not sorry."

"I forgive you anyway," said Harper. "I'm sorry for you. Truly confident people never have to bully, lie, steal or cheat to feel sure of themselves. I think you need more confidence."

"Yes," said Kirsty in a soft voice. "He just doesn't have the confidence to ask for help."

Jack Frost was darting furious looks at them all. Harper reached out and took his cold, bony fingers in her warm hand.

"When you give me my poise purse, I will give you something very special," she said. "Will you trust me, Jack Frost?"

Jack Frost stared into Harper's smiling face … and then turned and ran out of the cave.

Chapter Fifteen
Confidence Restored

What came next happened so fast that it made their heads spin. The dragon shot out of the cave like an arrow, swivelled in mid-air and landed in front of Jack Frost with a *ROAR*. The Ice Lord squealed and fell on his bottom. The fairies flew out of the cave and landed beside the dragon.

"Please listen," said Harper. "I've been watching you from my Confidence Lab and I've made something special for you."

Jack Frost opened the purse and peered into it with one beady eye.

"What is it?" he demanded. "I can't see anything in here."

"Only I know how my purse is organised," said Harper. "You'll never be able to find your gift."

Jack Frost held the poise purse upside down and shook it. He poked his nose into it and sniffed.

"You're fibbing," he said. "There's nothing in here."

Harper

"I never tell lies," said Harper. "There are lots of things in the purse, but you have to know where to look."

"Prove it," said Jack Frost, and he shoved the purse into her hands.

Harper smiled, and then put her hand into the purse.

"See, it's empty," Jack Frost snapped, folding his arms.

Harper's whole hand disappeared into the purse. Then her forearm … then her entire arm reached inside, all the way up to her shoulder. Rachel and Kirsty watched in amazement.

"Almost – got – it," Harper said, straining. "There!"

She pulled out her hand, closed in a fist. Then she uncurled her fingers, and everyone gasped, even the dragon.

An ice-blue hairclip lay in her palm, glittering so brightly with frosted silver beads that it dazzled their eyes. Jack Frost snatched it and clipped it into his spiky white hair.

"Mine," he shouted.

"You will still have to work on your own confidence," Harper told him. "My magic cannot totally create it for you. But this hairclip will make each spark of confidence ten times stronger."

Jack Frost turned to leave, and then paused. Slowly, he looked back over his shoulder at the Confidence Fairy.

"Thank you," he mumbled.

The words sounded strange coming out of his mouth. He looked a little embarrassed, but also pleased.

"It suits you," said Rachel in a friendly tone.

At this, Jack Frost looked even more pleased.

"I want to see for myself," he said. "I'm going back to my castle to look in the mirror."

There was a clap of thunder so loud that it made the dragon jump, and Jack Frost disappeared.

"Goodness me," said Kirsty. "Harper, I think you've just turned him into a nicer person."

The Confidence Fairy laughed.

"Even if it only lasts for a short while, it's a success," she said. "But the biggest success of all has been meeting you and working together."

They all hugged, the dragon wrapping her long scaly tail around them. Then Harper took out her wand.

"Shall I return you to your room in

Tippington?" she asked Rachel.

Rachel and Kirsty exchanged a glance and then shook their heads.

"I don't need to change my clothes for the party," said Kirsty. "I can feel my confidence flooding back."

"Me too," said Rachel. "We'll be happy in our ordinary clothes. Whatever we're wearing will look great as long as we feel good on the inside."

"That's the beauty of confidence," said Harper. "Thank you both for all your help today. I hope we meet again soon."

"Aren't you coming to the party?" Kirsty asked.

"No," said Harper. "I am going to teach some goblins how to communicate with the lonely dragon!"

She waved her wand, and the glow of

the Fire Mountains seemed to dwindle until they were only tiny, shining dots. Rachel and Kirsty blinked. They were back at the party, and the shining dots were the fairy lights in the trees.

"There you are," said Flora, pouncing on them. "Girls, it's going so well! People have been incredibly generous. I really feel confident that we can succeed."

"Of course we can," said Kirsty at once. "Shall we take over at the donations table now?"

The evening got better and better. Hundreds of local people turned up, eager to help the children. The best moment came when the clubhouse owner arrived. He was amazed when he saw how hard the children had worked.

"I wouldn't have had the confidence to do something like this when I was a boy," he told them. "I think you are all splendid, and I have decided to accept whatever you have raised as payment. The clubhouse is yours."

The children went wild with happiness. Rachel, Kirsty, Flora and Luca spun Sully's wheelchair and danced around him, while Rachel and Kirsty clapped and cheered. The band played louder than ever.

"I wish someone would invent a

confidence-o-meter," said Sully, when he got his breath back. "I think we'd all get a top score tonight!"

Everyone laughed, and Rachel and Kirsty exchanged a happy smile.

"After today's adventure, I know that we can do anything when we're together," said Rachel.

"Me too," Kirsty agreed. "No matter what Jack Frost does, he will never, ever shake my confidence in our friendship!"

The End

Now it's time for Kirsty and
Rachel to help ...

The Festive Fairies

Read on for a sneak peek ...

"Kirsty, it's snowing!" Rachel Walker
exclaimed with delight as she opened
the front door.

Kirsty Tate, Rachel's best friend,
peered outside to see large snowflakes
falling steadily.

"Brilliant!" Kirsty beamed, picking
up her gloves. "I hope it's snowing back
home, too."

Kirsty was staying with Rachel in
Tippington for a few days before
returning home on Christmas Eve.

"Maybe we're going to have a white
Christmas!" Rachel sighed happily,

wrapping her scarf snugly round her neck and picking up the bundle of Christmas cards her mum had asked her to post. "Come on, Kirsty."

Read the Festive Fairies Collection to find out what adventures are in store for Kirsty and Rachel!

Calling all parents, carers and teachers!
The Rainbow Magic fairies are here to help
your child enter the magical world of reading.
Whatever reading stage they are at, there's
a Rainbow Magic book for everyone!
Here is Lydia the Reading Fairy's guide to
supporting your child's journey at all levels.

Starting Out

Our Rainbow Magic Beginner Readers are perfect for first-time readers who are just beginning to develop reading skills and confidence. Approved by teachers, they contain a full range of educational levelling, as well as lively full-colour illustrations.

Developing Readers

Rainbow Magic Early Readers contain longer stories and wider vocabulary for building stamina and growing confidence. These are adaptations of our most popular Rainbow Magic stories, specially developed for younger readers in conjunction with an Early Years reading consultant, with full-colour illustrations.

Going Solo

The Rainbow Magic chapter books – a mixture of series and one-off specials – contain accessible writing to encourage your child to venture into reading independently. These highly collectible and much-loved magical stories inspire a love of reading to last a lifetime.

www.orchardseriesbooks.co.uk

"Rainbow Magic got my daughter reading chapter books. Great sparkly covers, cute fairies and traditional stories full of magic that she found impossible to put down" - Mother of Edie (6 years)

"Florence LOVES the Rainbow Magic books. She really enjoys reading now" - Mother of Florence (6 years)

Read along the Reading Rainbow!

Well done – you have completed the book!

This book was worth 2 stars.

See how far you have climbed on the Reading Rainbow opposite.
The more books you read, the more stars you can colour in
and the closer you will be to becoming a Royal Fairy!

Do you want to print your own Reading Rainbow?

1) Go to the Rainbow Magic website

2) Download and print out the poster

3) Colour in a star for every book you finish
and climb the Reading Rainbow

4) For every step up the rainbow,
you can download your very own certificate

There's all this and lots more at
orchardseriesbooks.co.uk

You'll find activities, stories, a special newsletter
AND you can search for the fairy with your name!